P9-DHB-777

The Night the Scarecrow Walked

For
James Sunderland MacNaught
when he is old enough to read

Text copyright © 1979 Natalie Savage Carlson.
Illustrations copyright © 1979 Charles Robinson.

Library of Congress Cataloging in Publication Data
Carlson, Natalie Savage
The night the scarecrow walked.
SUMMARY: Two children who sympathize with a
scarecrow that stands day after day in its field have
an opportunity to regret their interest.
[1. Scarecrows — Fiction. 2. Halloween — Fiction]
I. Robinson, Charles, 1931   II. Title.
PZ7.C2167Ni [E]   79-17320
ISBN 0-684-16311-X

This book published simultaneously in the United States
of America and Canada.
Copyright under the Berne Convention
All rights reserved. No part of this book may be reproduced in
any form without the permission of Charles Scribner's Sons.

Printed in the United States of America.
1 3 5 7 9 11 13 15 17 19 RD/C 20 18 16 14 12 10 8 6 4 2

The Night the Scarecrow Walked

by Natalie Savage Carlson

illustrated by Charles Robinson

Charles Scribner's Sons · New York

MAR 1980
JEFFERSONVILLE TOWNSHIP PUBLIC LIBRARY
JEFFERSONVILLE, INDIANA 47130

Eight-year-old Jeff and his little sister, Libby Lou, passed the cornfield every day on their way to and from school in the village. And they always stopped by the low stone wall to look at the scarecrow standing among the dry stubble.

He was a skinny scarecrow in a long ragged coat. The wide, shapeless brim of his stained felt hat hung low over where his face should have been.

"He must be tired of standing in one place all the time," said Libby Lou one day. "Now that the corn is in the shed, he doesn't even have the crows to scare away."

"Silly!" scoffed Jeff. "Scarecrows don't get tired of anything. They aren't real people."

"But he *looks* tired of standing there with nothing to do," insisted Libby Lou. "I bet he would like to walk out of that cornfield and *see* what the rest of the world is like."

"Tonight is Halloween," Jeff reminded her. "Maybe the ghosts and witches will take him for a ride with them."

"We can show him our jack-o'-lantern," said Libby Lou. "That might cheer him up even if he can't leave the field."

Each Halloween their mother picked a special pumpkin and scooped out the insides. Then Jeff and Libby Lou cut out the eyes, nose, and mouth, and Libby Lou lit the candle inside. At that instant, the pumpkin broke into a bright, warm smile.

Jeff and Libby Lou would walk to the village with the jack-o'-lantern and hold it up to Aunt Jane's window to scare her into giving them home-made doughnuts and cider.

So that evening, Mother and the children worked busily to bring the brightest, warmest grin to the pumpkin's face.

"Keep to the road," warned Mother. "You never know who might be up to mischief on Halloween night."

The children promised to take her advice. They started down the road.

It was a fit night for ghosts and witches. The pale moon looked like the ghost of a dead planet. Formless shadows moved across the road as if trying to block the children's path. Their own shadows followed fearfully, clinging to their heels. An owl moaned from a nearby oak tree. The branches creaked eerily. The children's shadows drew closer and closer together. Only the cheery grin on the pumpkin's face gave them courage to go on.

Soon they reached the stone wall of the cornfield. They looked across it. Jeff held the pumpkin
high for the scarecrow to see. But a dark cloud slid
across the face of the moon.

When it had passed, Jeff stiffened.

"L—look!" he exclaimed in a frightened whisper.

Libby Lou stared through the moonlight. A tall, lanky figure stepped from the scarecrow's post. It was draped in a long, loose coat and the floppy brim of a hat fell over its face. It slowly stalked across the stubble.

"The scarecrow!" Libby Lou whispered back.

She clutched Jeff's arm and the pumpkin's smile flickered.

The weird figure moved toward the wall below them with stiff, jerky steps. It clumsily climbed over the stones. It started up the road toward them.

"The scarecrow is coming after us!" cried Libby
Lou.

Jeff dropped the pumpkin. It fell with a dull thud and its grin disappeared. The children froze with fright. There was no light but that of the ghostly moon. There was no movement except that of the gaunt figure coming closer and closer.

Then Jeff and Libby Lou screamed. The
screams loosened their legs. They turned and raced
homeward. Their screams drowned out the hoots
of the owl.

Mother met them at the door. Her own face was pale under the porch light.

"What's wrong?" she cried. "What has happened?"

"The scarecrow!" panted Libby Lou.

"He walked out of the field," said Jeff breathlessly.

"He chased us!" cried Libby Lou.

Mother relaxed and laughed.

"It was probably just the shadows of the trees," she said. "Things do look scary on Halloween."

"No," said Jeff. "The scarecrow really walked out of the field and came after us."

"I'm not going to Aunt Jane's tonight," declared Libby Lou with a shiver.

"It's all your fault," accused Jeff. "He heard you wishing he could leave the cornfield."

"But I didn't mean on Halloween when everything is so spooky," said Libby Lou.

Mother led them inside.

"Then stay home and we'll have our own doughnuts and cider," she said.

So they did just that, and even bobbed for apples before they went to bed.

Next morning dawned clear and crisp. Only the sun made shadows and the owl was asleep in the oak tree.

"I'm not afraid of the scarecrow today," said Libby Lou. "He's probably back in his place."

Mother paused by the window.

"Who is that coming up the road?" she said.

The children went out on the porch.
Jeff suddenly leaned forward.
"Look!" he cried.

A skinny man in a long ragged coat was coming along with stiff, jerky steps. He was hunched forward with the wide brim of a stained felt hat flopping over his face.

As he neared the porch, he raised the brim and gave the children a gap-toothed, jack-o'-lantern grin. Then he squawked, "Caw, caw, caw!"

Jeff and Libby Lou stared at each other.

"The scarecrow!" exclaimed Libby Lou.

"Come!" cried her brother. "Let's find out."

Jeff jumped off the porch and Libby Lou caught up with him on the road. They ran all the way to the cornfield. They stopped by the stone wall.

The scarecrow was gone. Only two crossed sticks marked the place where he had stood.

For a few moments, the children couldn't speak.

"It really was the scarecrow," said Libby Lou in an awed voice. "He got so tired of that field that he decided to leave it and see the world."

"No, silly!" scoffed Jeff. "That was a man that we saw walking just now. He must have helped himself to the scarecrow's clothes last night."

Libby Lou stubbornly shook her head.

"I know it was the scarecrow," she insisted, "and I'm glad he got out of the field even if he did scare us more than the crows."

Jeff mulled over this for a few seconds.

"Maybe," he half agreed. "I guess anything could happen on Halloween."

CARLSON, NATALIE SAVAGE
THE NIGHT THE SCARECROW WALKED
je   80-02586

3 1861 00238 5902

JEFFERSONVILLE TOWNSHIP
PUBLIC LIBRARY
P. O. BOX 548
JEFFERSONVILLE, INDIANA 47130